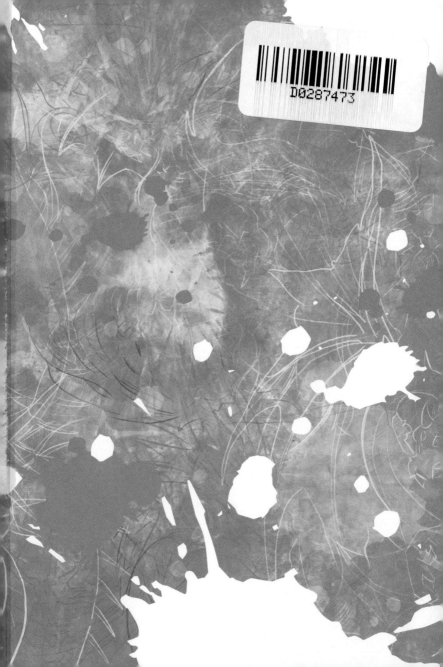

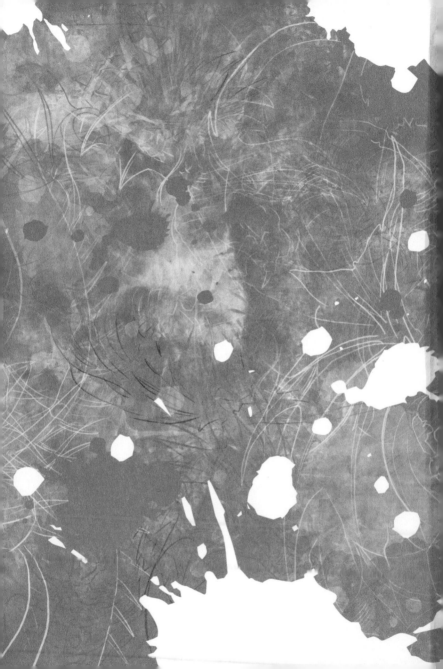

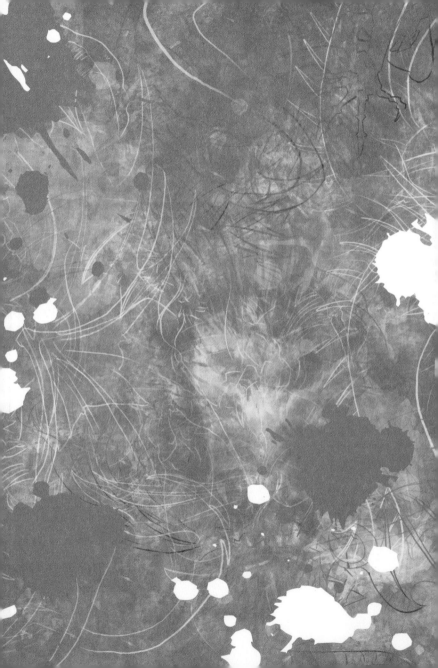

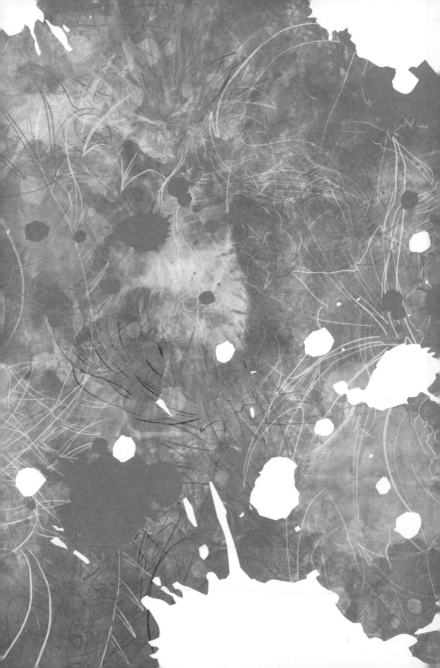

DRAGONBLOOD
STOWAWAY MONSTER

Michael Dahl

Richard Pellegrino

STONE ARCH BOOKS
www.stonearchbooks.com

Zone Books are published by
Stone Arch Books
A Capstone Imprint
1710 Roe Crest Drive
North Mankato, Minnesota 56003
www.capstonepub.com

Library of Congress Cataloging-in-Publication Data
Dahl, Michael.
    Stowaway Monster / by Michael Dahl; illustrated by
Richard Pellegrino.
    p. cm. — (Zone Books. Dragonblood)
    ISBN 978-1-4342-1259-7 (library binding)
    ISBN 978-1-4342-2312-8 (softcover)
    [1. Dragons—Fiction. 2. Stowaways—Fiction.] I.
Pellegrino, Richard, 1980– ill. II. Title.
PZ7.D15134St 2009
[Fic]—dc22   2008031283

Summary: Eli is a young stowaway on a ship bound for
North America. A strange birthmark on his arm, in the
shape of a dragon, begins to sting. Then he meets a
sailor on the ship with a dragon tattoo. The tattoo, and
a weird cargo hidden on the ship, hold the secret to Eli's
real identity.

Creative Director: Heather Kindseth
Graphic Designer: Brann Garvey

Printed in the United States of America in North Mankato, Minnesota.
072012
006846R

TABLE OF CONTENTS

Introduction

A new Age of Dragons is about to begin. The **powerful** creatures will return to rule the **world** once more, but this time will be **different**. This time, they will have allies. Who will **help** them? Around the world, some young humans are making a strange **discovery**. They are learning that they were born with **dragon blood** – blood that gives them **amazing powers**.

CHAPTER 1
The Stowaway

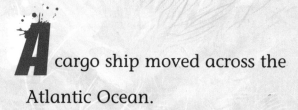

A cargo ship moved across the Atlantic Ocean.

 **Dark clouds** filled the sky.

Dark waves slapped against the ship's metal hull.

Eli hid on the ship. He was a **stowaway.**

Quietly, Eli stepped out from his hiding place.

A man's hand reached out from the darkness and grabbed Eli's arm.

CHAPTER 2

The Tattoo

"What are you doing here?" growled the older man. He was a sailor on the ship.

Eli froze. "I want to go to America," he said. "I want to work. I want a new life."

The man stared hard at Eli.

"Don't worry," the man said. "I understand."

Eli stared at the man's arm.

The skin was covered with a wild,

colorful **tattoo**.

It was a flying **dragon**.

The man looked around to
make sure no one was watching.

Then he said, "Come with me. We need to get you something to eat."

Eli relaxed. Then he followed the man through a storeroom.

He felt grateful to the older man. He was also confused.

The **dragon** tattoo reminded him of something.

The man's tattoo looked like the birthmark Eli had on his own arm.

CHAPTER 3
The Locked Door

The sailor led Eli below the ship's decks.

They walked down several sets of metal stairs.

Eli could feel the ship move when the dark waves slapped against its side.

They passed a metal door. There was a sign on the door. It read: Cargo Room.

The man turned to Eli and said, "That room is off limits. No one goes in there but the captain."

Eli passed by the door.

His arm felt strange. The birthmark felt as if it was burning his skin.

When the door was behind him,
the burning feeling went away.

CHAPTER 4
A Trick?

Inside a room, the sailor gave Eli a bowl of soup.

"I know what it's like to leave your home behind," said the man. "I wanted a new life too."

"Just make sure no one sees you," he warned Eli. "I'll get you off the ship when we reach port."

Eli slept in a bunk above the man's bed.

In the middle of the night, a noise woke him.

The man was leaving the cabin.

As soon as the door closed, Eli
jumped out of his bunk.

He wondered if the man had
tricked him.

Would the man bring the
captain? Would they arrest Eli for
hiding on the ship?

Eli left the cabin. He hurried back toward the metal steps.

Suddenly, he stopped.

The sailor was walking through the door marked **Cargo Room.**

"What's he doing?" Eli *whispered.*

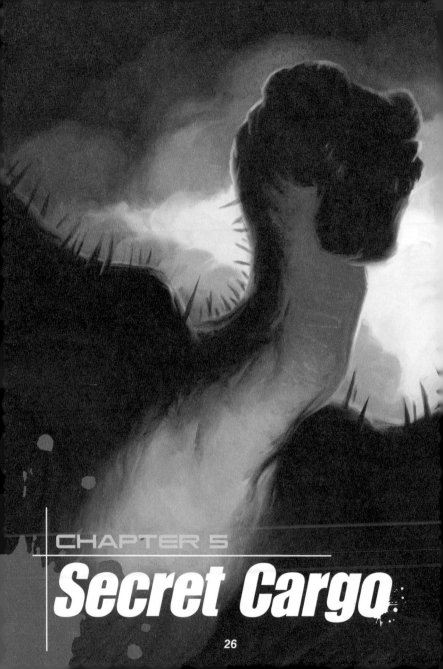

CHAPTER 5
Secret Cargo

Eli followed the man into the forbidden room. His birthmark began to burn again.

Deep inside the dark room, Eli saw the man.

The man was staring at open wooden boxes.

He raised his arms above his head and shouted, "No!"

The wooden boxes were full of eggs.

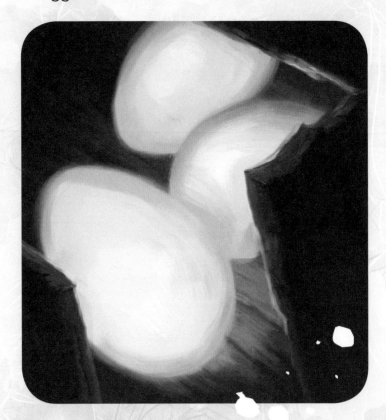

Gigantic eggs!

"These do not belong to humans!" cried the man. "They should be free!"

Eli felt a warm breeze. A flash of light blinded him.

Then he blinked his eyes. The man had changed. Instead of a man standing in the darkness, there was a dragon with wings.

Flames shot from the **dragon's** mouth.

The flames melted the metal wall of the room. Eli could see the night sky through the opening.

Then the **dragon** flapped its wings.

The breeze from the *wings* blew the boxes and eggs through the wall. They fell into the ocean.

The dragon turned and looked at Eli. It flashed its teeth.

"You are one of us," growled the dragon.

Spreading its wings, the dragon flew through the opening and was gone.

"Who are you?" yelled Eli.

Eli's birthmark suddenly felt like *ice*.

Color began to seep into the
edges of the birthmark. Now it
looked even more like the man's
dragon tattoo.

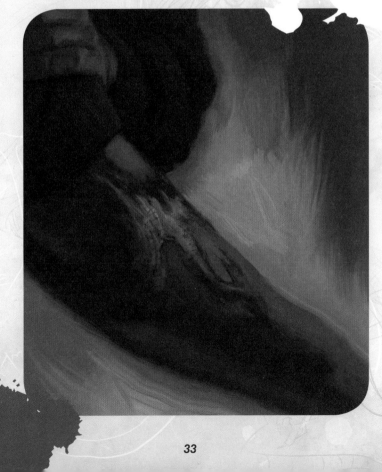

Of Dragons and Near-Dragons

Reptile eggs always start out white. Many
reptile eggs are rubbery. The eggs of turtles,
geckos, and some other species are hard.
The eggs of snakes and most lizards are
softer and feel like leather.

Most reptiles lay eggs. However, some
species of reptiles deliver live young.

In the species that lay eggs, the female digs
a hole. She puts the eggs into the hole and
buries them. This helps protect the eggs
from predators.

In the wild, reptile eggs are usually buried. In captivity, eggs are placed in an **incubator** (ING-kyuh-bay-tur). This machine keeps eggs warm until they hatch.

Reptile eggs have many predators, including other reptiles. The African egg-eating snake will swallow another egg whole. Then it cracks the egg open and swallows the contents. In the end, it will spit out the egg shell in one piece.

The leatherback turtle is the world's largest reptile. Females can lay as many as 1,000 eggs in one season!

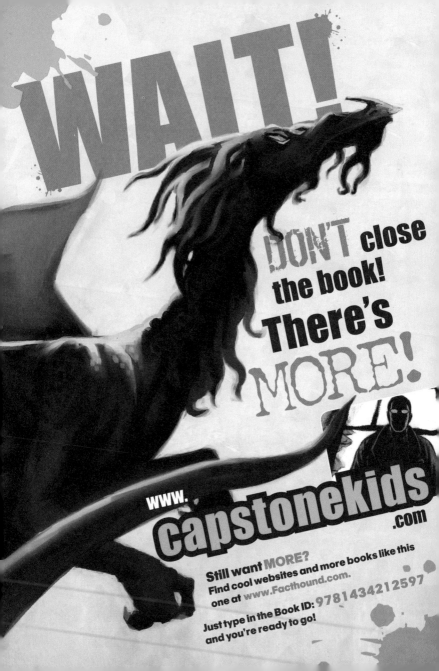

GLOSSARY

allies (AL-eyez)—people or countries that give support to each other

birthmark (BURTH-mark)—a mark on the skin that was there from birth

creature (KREE-chur)—a living thing that is human or animal

forbidden (fawr-BID-en)—when something is off limits or entry is not allowed

grateful (GRAYT-fuhl)—thankful and appreciative

hull (HUHL)—the frame or body of a boat or ship

rule (ROOL)—have power over something

seep (SEEP)—to flow or trickle slowly

stowaway (STOH-uh-way)—someone who hides in a plane, ship, or boat to avoid paying for the trip

DISCUSSION QUESTIONS

1. Do you think it was right for Eli to sneak onto the cargo ship? Why or why not?

2. Why did Eli's arm burn when he walked by the cargo room?

3. Why do you think the old man was nice to Eli right away?

WRITING PROMPTS

1. Do you think the old man was a good or bad guy? Write a paragraph explaining your answer.

2. Were you surprised by the ending? Explain your answer in a written paragraph.

3. What do you think happens to Eli after the dragon flies away? Write another chapter to the story. Be sure to include what happens to the old man too.

INTERNET SITES

The book may be over, but the adventure is just beginning.

Do you want to read more about the subjects or ideas in this book? Want to play cool games or watch videos about the authors who write these books? Then go to FactHound. At *www.facthound.com,* you'll be able to do all that, and more. The FactHound website can also send you to other safe Internet sites.

Check it out!

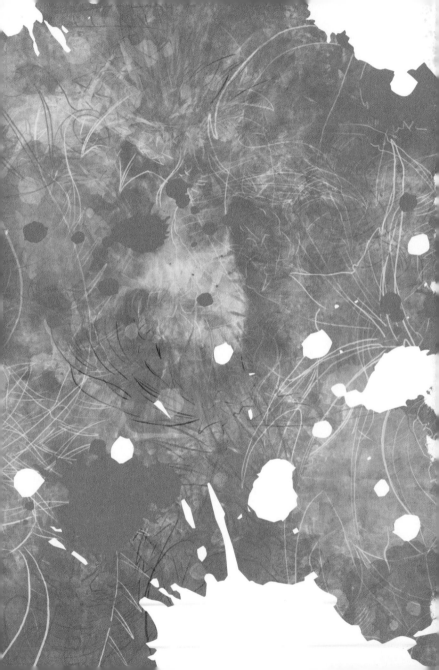

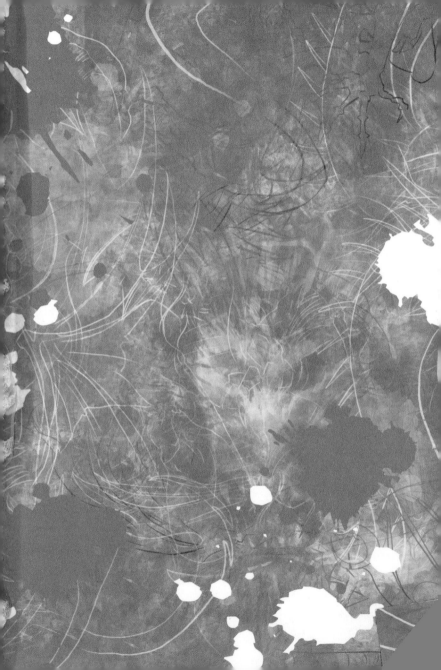

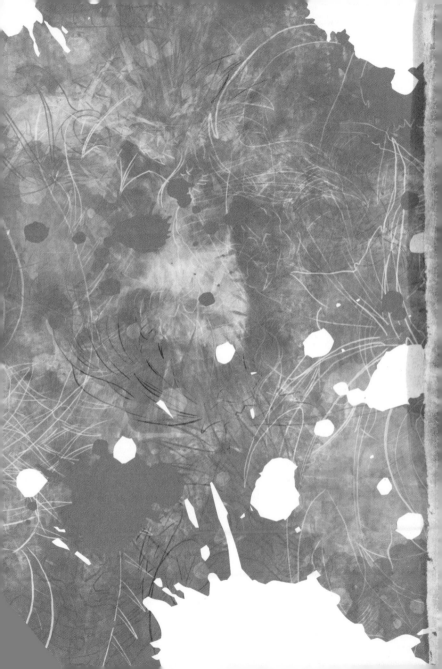